© for the German edition: 2022,
Verlagshaus Jacoby & Stuart GmbH, Berlin, Germany
Under the title: *Ich hab doch keine Angst!*
(Der große und der kleine Igel)
© text and illustrations: Britta Teckentrup
© for the English edition: 2023,
Prestel Verlag, Munich · London · New York
A member of Penguin Random House
Verlagsgruppe GmbH
Neumarkter Strasse 28 · 81673 Munich

Library of Congress Control Number: 2022944656
A CIP catalogue record for this book is available
from the British Library.

Translated from the German by Nicola Stuart

Copyediting: Brad Finger
Production management and typesetting:
Susanne Hermann
Printing and binding: TBB, a.s.

Prestel Publishing compensates the CO_2 emissions
produced from the making of this book by supporting
a reforestation project in Brazil.
Find further information on the project here:
www.ClimatePartner.com/14044-1912-1001

Penguin Random House Verlagsgruppe
FSC® N001967

Printed in Slovakia

ISBN 978-3-7913-7541-0
www.prestel.com

Britta Teckentrup

I'm Not Scared

A Big Hedgehog and Little Hedgehog Adventure

PRESTEL

Munich · London · New York

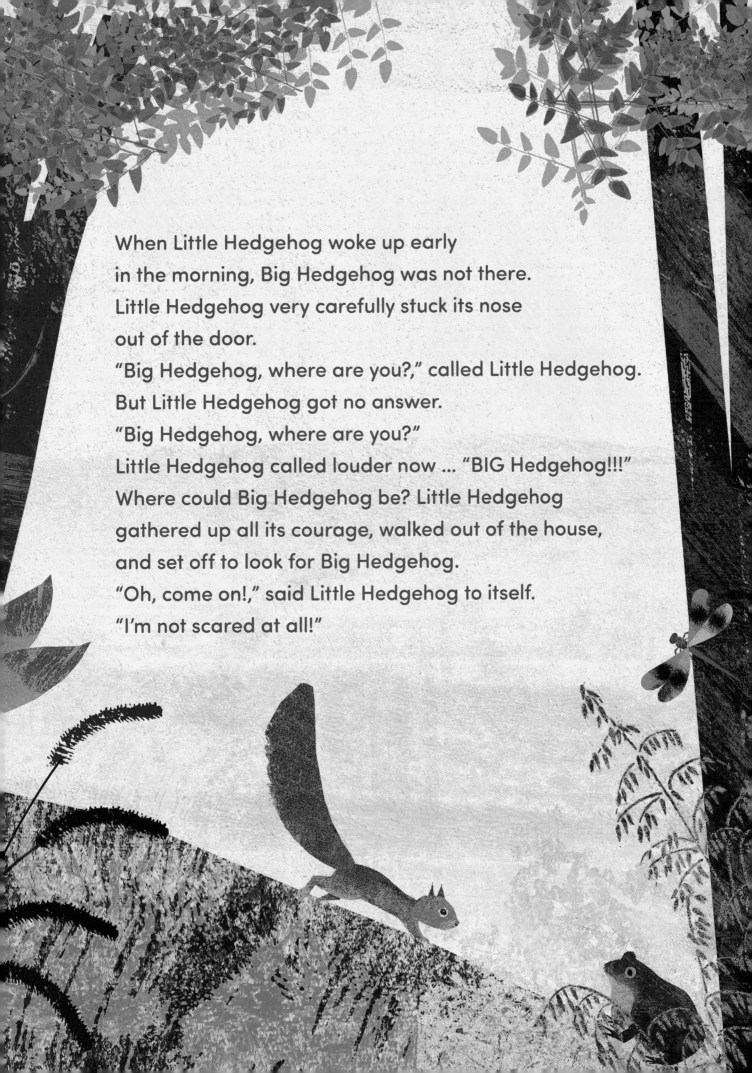

When Little Hedgehog woke up early
in the morning, Big Hedgehog was not there.
Little Hedgehog very carefully stuck its nose
out of the door.
"Big Hedgehog, where are you?," called Little Hedgehog.
But Little Hedgehog got no answer.
"Big Hedgehog, where are you?"
Little Hedgehog called louder now ... "BIG Hedgehog!!!"
Where could Big Hedgehog be? Little Hedgehog
gathered up all its courage, walked out of the house,
and set off to look for Big Hedgehog.
"Oh, come on!," said Little Hedgehog to itself.
"I'm not scared at all!"

Little Hedgehog searched behind the house, on the roof, under the bushes, and went around the massive old tree, but Big Hedgehog was nowhere to be found. Little Hedgehog felt very uncomfortable.

Then Little Hedgehog heard a noise from the basement.

Maybe Big Hedgehog was down there? But Little Hedgehog didn't like going into the basement, because it was so dark down there. "Oh, come on, I'm not scared at all!" Little Hedgehog encouraged itself and began walking down the stairs very, very slowly ...

"Good morning, Little Hedgehog. You are already awake!"
Big Hedgehog was just coming up the stairs.
"What are you doing here? Were you afraid that I was gone because
you couldn't find me?"
Little Hedgehog was beaming with joy that Big Hedgehog was back.

"Oh, come on, I knew you had to be here in the basement.
I was just coming down to get you. I wasn't scared at all!"
"Look, Little Hedgehog, I've packed a picnic basket for us.
Let's go on an adventure trip together!"

Little Hedgehog loved adventures, and the two set off
together. First, they walked into the forest.
Little Hedgehog actually liked the forest, but sometimes
found it a bit scary there.
Big Hedgehog began to whistle a song,
and Little Hedgehog whistled along.
Little Hedgehog couldn't whistle very well yet,
but did its best anyway.
The two of them walked – happily whistling –
through the forest.
But when their song was over, the whistling continued.
Big Hedgehog and Little Hedgehog looked
at each other with wide eyes.
"Is that you, Little Hedgehog?," asked Big Hedgehog.
"Is that you, Big Hedgehog?," asked Little Hedgehog.
"If it's not us, who is whistling our song?,"
they said at the same time.
The whistling came from high above them
in the trees.
It grew louder and louder, until it whistled
from all sides. Little Hedgehog hid behind
Big Hedgehog and looked up.
It was really scary.

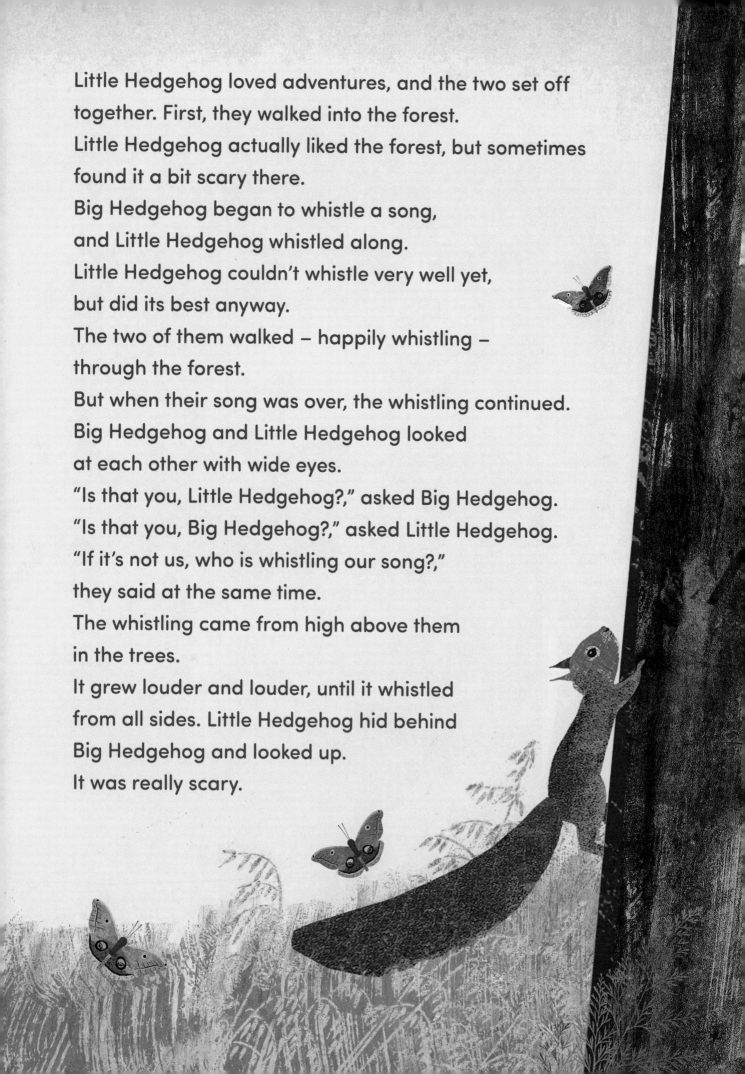

Suddenly, a flock of colorful birds flew out of
the trees. The birds settled down next to
Big Hedgehog and Little Hedgehog.
"Your song was so beautiful, we just had to
whistle along. But we didn't want to scare you.
Sorry, Little Hedgehog!"
And with a whoosh, all the birds flew back up
into the trees.

"Oh, come on, I wasn't scared!,"
Little Hedgehog called after them.

Big Hedgehog and Little Hedgehog took each other by the hand and continued walking through the forest.

They took ten steps forward and five steps back, ten steps forward and five steps back: 1, 2, 3, 4, 5, 6, 7, 8, 9, 10.

1, 2, 3, 4, 5 ... All of a sudden, they noticed a penetrating smell directly behind them.
Big Hedgehog turned around very slowly ...

"HELP, A FOX!!!!"

"Roll up, Little Hedgehog, as fast as you can!," cried Big Hedgehog. The two hedgehogs rolled up so tightly that they looked like spiky balls. Little Hedgehog had been practicing this many times before at home. They then rolled down the slope together, over branches and stones and earth and roots. When they reached the bottom, their hearts were beating very fast, but they had shaken off the fox!

"Well done, Little Hedgehog. That was close. Were you as scared as I was?," asked Big Hedgehog. "Me? Oh, come on, I wasn't scared at all," mumbled Little Hedgehog in a slightly quivering voice. But it didn't sound quite convincing.

Big Hedgehog and Little Hedgehog looked around. In front of
them was a large meadow and the sun was laughing from the sky.
They played hide-and-seek, nestled down in the grass, enjoyed
the day, and forgot about time.

But they had nothing to eat. They were so scared when they
fled the fox, they had lost their basket in the forest.
Slowly, Big Hedgehog and Little Hedgehog got hungry.

They hadn't noticed the time, but it was getting quite late and it was time to go home.

Nor had they noticed the rising fog in which the meadow was suddenly bathed.

"Oh dear," said Big Hedgehog. "Which way do we have to go now?"

"There's light back there, let's go there!," called Little Hedgehog, pulling Big Hedgehog's hand.

But the light was getting brighter and brighter and bigger ... and louder and louder!

"That's ... that's ... A CAR!," cried Big Hedgehog.

"Watch out, Little Hedgehog!"

Big Hedgehog pulled Little Hedgehog into the bushes.

"Phew, that was close, Little Hedgehog. You must have been scared stiff!"

Little Hedgehog looked at Big Hedgehog with its eyes wide open and said in a shaky voice: "But I wasn't scared at all, Big Hedgehog! Well, not really anyway. Or maybe just a little ... no, not a bit ..."

Little Hedgehog breathed deeply.

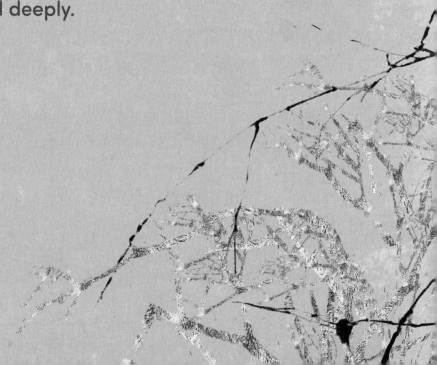

When they saw the houses, Big Hedgehog realized they had
walked the wrong way through the thick fog ...
"Meow!"
Little Hedgehog hid behind Big Hedgehog.
"Meow!!!" Big Hedgehog knew exactly who this voice belonged to:
Black Cat.

The two had known each other for a long time and were friends.
"What are you doing here, so far away from your home?,"
asked Black Cat. They told their friend about all of their adventures,
and about how they had gotten lost in the fog and mist.
"You must have been very scared, Little Hedgehog!"
"Oh, no, I wasn't scared at all!," Little Hedgehog said boastfully.

"Come on, I'll take you home!," said Black
Cat. "I know the way. Just climb on my back.
You must be tired, Little Hedgehog."
"Not me!," replied Little Hedgehog, a little
offended, and climbed onto the cat's back.

"Big Hedgehog," whispered Little
Hedgehog on their way home.
"Yes, Little Hedgehog."
"I WAS a tiny bit scared today after all."
Big Hedgehog smiled and pulled
Little Hedgehog a little closer. "I know,
Little Hedgehog, and that's just as well."

"Thank you, dear Black Cat," said Big Hedgehog
when they arrived home.

"Good night and sleep tight, Little Hedgehog," murmured
Black Cat. But Little Hedgehog could no longer answer,
as Little Hedgehog had already fallen fast asleep ...